Myrtle Reed

Love Letters of a Musician

Myrtle Reed

Love Letters of a Musician

ISBN/EAN: 9783337247829

Printed in Europe, USA, Canada, Australia, Japan

Cover: Foto ©Andreas Hilbeck / pixelio.de

More available books at **www.hansebooks.com**

LOVE LETTERS OF A MUSICIAN

By Myrtle Reed

G. P. PUTNAM'S SONS
New York and London
The Knickerbocker Press
1899

Contents

PART I

PART II

PART III

Contents

PART ONE

PART ONE

The Face in the Fire

Largo

The Face in the Fire

MY LADY :

I don't know just how to tell you what I Largo feel to-night, for I am little more than a boy and pretty badly confused, even for me. Your letter is all kindness and I can't tell you how much I appreciate it, though I cannot see what you have done that should make you ask me to forgive you. I have known for a long time how much I cared for you, but I thought I could manage to keep it to myself. I knew that to tell you would be but to hurt you—and you know I would not willingly do that.

You are not to blame if I care for you, nor am I, perhaps—but that unmerciful thing that people call Fate or Providence or God. And if there is a little of the bitter in it, there is much more that is sweet and good and beautiful—like you.

It makes me feel as if I were near you, to

write to you, and I can't bear to feel that you are so far away. You know all that I would tell you, and you know that in loving you I love my ideal—not merely a woman.

There is one bright spot that makes all the gloomy world seem bright. I have n't lost you ! I have n't lost you ! For you said you would be my friend all your life, even though I did n't see you. That is best, no doubt, for you know. But you are so vividly present with me that in writing to you I am doing little more than talking to myself, and you need never know, my Lady, that I have written.

Strange fancy, is it not ? To write as if to a sweetheart, to one who has promised to be my friend, but why need it matter, if the letters are not sent ? I shall please myself by dreaming that they reach you, even if they are posted in the strangest of places—my trunk ! I am going to cut a slit in the side, like a real letter-box, and put a box inside to hold them. Then, when I have sent a letter to you, I can go on about my work. I shall always look for the answer, though the postman seldom comes my way, and always, dear,

I shall love you, though you do not write nor know.

I want you—just as though I had not given you up and that by your own command. I would try hard to win you, if I had the right to try. But you are not for me—a wandering musician, with only a violin between him and poverty,—hardship was never meant for such as you. And it would be that with me, try as I would to shield you.

The winter outside to-night is no colder than that within my heart. Life stretches out before me like a bare, vast plain. But in fancy I shall have you with me until the plain is crossed, and I reach the open, unknown sea.

There is a fire on my hearthstone to-night and in the flickering flame I see a woman's face. No need to ask what face it is, for to me there is only one—tender brown eyes, soft hair, and lips so divinely dear that I love them, even though they have said "no" to the question that held my heart within it.

The fire changes from rose to gold and I see you in your different moods—you have as many as an April day. Sometimes you are radiant and queenly, sometimes scornful, sometimes merry or serious, sometimes tender—but behind all the moods I see the one woman, with the one crown—womanhood.

You would laugh if you could see my little attic chamber, with only the fire and a single candle for light. But would you laugh? Perhaps your eyes would fill with tender pity, for I remember that I saw them thus, only last night when I told you that I loved you.

I am twenty-five and you are twenty-one, and I have loved you four years and never told you. We have been comrades, chums, whatever you will—ah, little girl, do you think there has been no need for self-control? And I have had but one dream of you—a vain one.

The firelight makes your face tender now, and your eyes thrill me with their sweet seriousness. I would not exchange that fire for the palace of a king, since it enshrines your face. The gold of it is your soul, the rose of it your heart, and the warmth and glory of it your love, which waits for someone.

But you shall be as fully mine as his, through my journey across the treeless plain. And at the last, when I reach the shore of the soundless sea, I shall look back once to your face, as I see it in the fire now.   God bless you, dear, and good-night, and—no, just good-night.

A Dream

Maestoso

CAVATINA   RAFF

A Dream

THE snow is deep on the ground to-night, dear Lady, and the day has been hard for me. It is only at night in my own room that I can think of you, for the world jars upon the music that goes out from my soul to yours.

I am first violin in a theatre orchestra this week and the play is a melodrama, of the pitiful, pathetic kind. There is no room for Art and it is not Nature—rather a travesty upon both. But we need not speak of this.

Last night I dreamed of you, not for the first time, as you may guess. I thought I had won you and then lost you, but it was given me to follow you, in the path of the Angel who held you fast.

It was a wonderful journey through the still air—through cold and trackless blue, past flaming suns and tender stars, among countless meteors that changed dark to day, among the illimitable midnights of the universe, and

A Dream

away from the far-off Earth, where men and women love and suffer, and at the best can only pray.

But I saw no star-fields like those eyes of yours, my Heart, and I followed untiringly the grey, shadowy mist that enveloped you, until we reached an endless plain of night. I could not see you, yet I went on until I grew so weary I could go no farther. Then there was a faint glimmer through the dark, it grew brighter and brighter—then dawn! and I held you in my arms.

But no dream like that can atone for the glory I have missed—of holding you. Did you ever think, my Lady, that in all these years I have never touched you once, save to take your hand in greeting and farewell?

Once, I think, you would not have minded. You asked me to play to you and I chose the "Cavatina." It was not Raff who thrilled you that night—it was I. My story was in the music—all the love and longing and waiting—and I thought you understood. Your lips were parted, your eyes were shining— ah, Love, had I dared to claim you at the moment you were mine!

I want no unwilling surrender. I would not lead you, queen as you are, to a half-hearted slavery, even of the sweetest kind. Yet, had I dared—but no memory of your lips could be more real than my dream of them.

Fate may deny me love, but not loving. The honor of it is not yours, but mine—I am proud that I am man enough to love you.

Philosophy avails little when the heart cuts and burns and stings, and, try as I may, I cannot mask the bitter truth. Do you see the funny little spots all over the page? They are tears—men have no power to wring them from me, but you——

Oh, Sweetheart, Sweetheart, Sweetheart! I will follow you through fire and cloud if I may only dream again!

The Sea and a Shell

Largo

18

The Sea and a Shell

BECAUSE I wanted to be alone with you, Largo I went down to the sea to-day, cold and bleak though it was, for I could not endure the city any longer. Have you ever seen it in winter? The two or three who passed me were shivering with the cold, but I bared my throat to the keen salt wind and exulted in it.

There is something in that field of unresting blue that always comforts me. It is like standing on the prairie at night with no light but the stars, and hearing the wind make melody through the harp-strings of the grass.

It seems as if there should be a tide on the prairie, it is so like the sea.

Beside the vastness of it, one's little self shrinks into nothingness, and, with it, one's little troubles. What room is there for a human sorrow beside anything so great as this? Why, you could take your heart in the hollow of your hand, it is so little a thing, and yet all the trouble in the world arises from it. There is room enough for all our joy, but it is neither wide enough nor deep enough to hold our pain.

Still, it is only through suffering that we grow, and when we suffer enough, we are great. When we can express it, we are artists, and when we cannot, we are only poor human children, stricken dumb with grief.

Do you remember Abelard and Heloise? He was going to reach a fame too great for her to share, and he lives only through the world's memory of that wronged woman's love.

I have been wondering to-day if this was given me for the sake of my music or if my music was given me for the sake of this. In the path of every great artist is an unfulfilled love, and yet I would gladly surrender my claim to earthly immortality for a heavenly mortality with you.

How much of the sonorous glory of Beethoven belongs to Adelaide? I believe that all of it was hers, after he began to love her, just as all my music shall be yours. Love makes a tide in the soul—the ebb is minor, the flow major, and the whole a symphony.

But what is the use of it all! I might cry out, but no one would hear. There is so much grief in the world that the sound of my voice would be drowned and lost, as one wave is deadened by the majestic chords of surf that crash superbly on the shore.

A storm was coming up to-day, and I watched it, sweeping down on grey wings from the north. A single gull sped in advance of it, strong, stately, and straight as an arrow, to some more kindly harbour. There were no fetters binding him to earth—he was free to sail through the measureless heaven or to breast the unmeasured sea. The waves are bound—surge and toss as they may, they belong to Earth for ever and ever, as until the last day of eternity, I belong to you, who are free as the gull.

There was a tiny shell at my feet and I picked it up. By holding it to my ear I heard the sound of the breakers, so divinely soft and sweet that it seemed like a dream.

There was no hint of storm in that far-off melody—only blue skies and tropic islands, sapphire depths of sea, and dazzling reaches of sunlight.   The little shell knew nothing of the tempests that sweep the waters and lash them into foam, nothing of shipwreck or loss. And so, if I had the appointment of it, your life would be.

Love is first a shield and then an uplifting, and in shielding you I should be uplifted myself.   There is no degree in loving; you must give all or none, and I have given all.

Dear Lady of my Heart, pain given by your hand becomes the keenest joy, because you have given it.   And since pain means so much, I dare not think what joy would be.

The Blind Spinner

Largo

SPINNING SONG

MENDELSSOHN

24

The Blind Spinner

Largo

A LITTLE web is in the corner of my room, which I have just found. I have been watching the tiny occupant as he builds his house around him, apparently without design and yet with the craftiest of intentions.

No matter how many times he is driven away or his house destroyed, he begins anew with each failure and outwardly with the same cheerfulness. It is not given us to fathom his mental process, but we who have built a House of Dreams, and seen it shattered at a single blow, can appreciate his feelings when he begins anew upon other foundations.

Within that tiny body dwells a wondrous chemistry. Who could trace the shimmering, shining web to the crude, misshapen thing that forms it? And who, knowing the Spinner, would not wish him a fortunate spinning?

I am a spinner too, but my web is Life.

The Blind Spinner

My room is the world, and in my little corner I make a fabric of dreams that any breath may blow aside. The threads are torn and broken and some are soiled, and sometimes I go up a little higher and begin again.

But I can never relay my first foundations. The guiding threads are fixed and eternal and the new web must always be constructed upon the old plan. Ah, the thousand aches and disappointments that go in with the weaving! No mistake can be corrected, no loss made good, after it is once done. The variation of a hair's breadth at the beginning makes a defect at the end, but I work on, all through my little day, unseeing, and hoping against hope.

It is a sombre grey, this web of Life, but it becomes silver when the light shines upon it, and in the sun it glows with rainbow hues. A broken, distorted web is beautiful then, and mine is broken in many places, though I have spun as best I may.

My love for you, dear Lady, is the light upon my web, and ill-shapen and shattered though it is, there lies within its meshes a human heart.

So I pray that He, seeing what lies within the imperfect tapestry, may forgive the Blind Spinner for his thousand mistakes, and deem the web not wholly unworthy of reward, for the sake of the Light which shines upon it.

The Blind Spinner

Goldenrod and Snow

Larghetto

29

LIEBLING

30

Goldenrod and Snow

TO-DAY, with its keen, crisp winter air, *Largbetto* has been so like the same day a year ago, that I have been out to the river, where we went when a childish fancy called you, even in the snow.

You used to say that I was the only one you knew who did not spoil the beauty of the woods for you. I longed to tell you that you made them beautiful for me, but I dared not. I have found out that you not only bring beauty with you, but the memory of you carries with it a subtle charm that makes a frozen stream a silver ribbon between two banks of pearl.

I lived it all over again to-day, walking alone where once we walked together, and finding the same clumps of dead goldenrod, weighted down with snow. You might as well have been with me, Sweet Lady of my Dreams, for the place was eloquent with your presence.

There seemed to be a hallowed path marked
out on the ice, where your feet had trod the
year before.   The silence was deeper there,
as if some holy thing had just gone by.

Last year I spoke of the dead flowers, and
you said, " They 're not dead—they 've just
gone to sleep."   Then you took your hand-
kerchief and brushed the snow from a tall
purple aster, that I might see how tightly the
dried petals had closed round the heart of the
flower.   You knew it was a purple aster, for
you know all the wood things by name, but I
could not have found one in the snow.

There were little webs in the grass along
the banks, close to the river, where the snow
had not fallen, marked out with silver and set
with stars of frost.   And there was no weed
that did not have its panoply of whiteness
and its attendant train of tiny pages stumbling
through the snow.   You found a haughty
burdock, pompous in his new majesty, and
pointed out a long, straggling line of train-
bearers, grown sleepy with their task.

Of a sudden, you remembered the purple
aster that you had left uncovered, and we had
to go back to it, while you sifted snow over

it, with a sweet seriousness on your face. In some ways, I think you will always be a child. Dear, white little soul, I could ask no greater thing from God than that He should keep you as you are.

I lingered by the river until sunset. You never know what a sunset can be until you see it in winter, behind the leafless trees. There were just clouds enough to make it beautiful, and I stood on the bluff above, where we waited for it so long ago.

Gold and purple and crimson and azure changed to opal and grey, far across a stretch of snowy plain. It was as if the Gates of Light had opened out upon Earth. And at the last, when it seemed as if I must turn to see that wondrous glow reflected in your face, something blinded my sight, and in a flood of molten glory which my wet eyes could not see, the sun went down.

The Tide of the Year

Larghetto

35

The Tide of the Year

IT is late now, but I cannot deny myself the *Larghetto* luxury of a talk with you. I am wondering what you would say if you were to see these letters—would you think me presuming and impertinent, or would you understand?

I have been reading to-day, in a little book you gave me long ago:

> " God be thanked, the meanest of his creatures
> Boasts two soul-sides—one to face the world with,
> One to show a woman when he loves her."

You will never see the side of my soul that loves you.   One part of my nature is reserved and cold, but the other—ah, my Heart ! not even you can know the warmth and tenderness of that.

All the best of me belongs to you.   There is no talent nor aspiration nor goodness in me that is not wholly yours.   And of you, I have memories and the assurance of your friendship.   I am not complaining—it is enough.

Drip, drip, drip—I can hear water dropping on the roof. The trees are giving up their weight of ice, and the bare boughs are turning in their sleep. That means spring.

What a tide it is—the ebb and flow of the year! The summer recedes, slowly, gradually, and leaves a little green, then scarlet, and finally grey. The earth is cold and white—summer is far south, waiting for the sun to summon her tide as the moon calls the waters.

You can almost see it when it comes in, with a rush and a joy that bursts into pink and white blossoming. It is a mating-call—robin and thrush and bluebird break into song and drink the new wine of the year.

Then there is summer. The wheat-fields turn from green to gold, and in the warm, sweet air a thousand singers speed on shining wing from field to field.

Then harvest. The tide is at flood now. See all the priceless things the incoming wave has brought! Fruit and grain and grasses—all these to last until it comes in again.

There is a little moment of rest before the turning, and they call it Indian Summer. The air is full of the mist of parting—the sad sweetness of it fills Earth with a gentle regret. No hesitancy marks its stately recessional; it goes farther and farther back upon the vast shore of the world, leaving its track bare and desolate. But we know it will come again.

Is there an ebb and flow in the heart, dear Lady? I think it must always be flood-tide there. But the heart is so small it can scarcely hold it.

It has not found you yet, and the waves do not know of the white, sweet shore that waits for their caressing. You are like the sleeping Princess, and your Prince is tarrying.

But when you wake, may God make it a happy dawn for you and not a night like this!

A Dream-Sweetheart

Andante amoroso

SERENADE

SCHUBERT

A Dream=Sweetheart

BECAUSE it is Sunday, I have been playing the things you like best and fancying you were here to listen. Your fingers were finding a dream accompaniment on a wholly imaginary piano, and we were so happy !.

We had tea together to-night, you and I. Instead of going out, I set my little table for two and drew a chair for you opposite mine. You would laugh at my housekeeping, but I did the best I could for my guest. There were none of the dainty little touches that women give—I fear even the most careless observer would know that a man had laid the table.

But you did not mind, dear Dream-Sweetheart, so why should I? We laughed and talked and your eyes danced with fun. The firelight was shining on your face and touching your hair with gold.

You wanted to help afterward, but I enthroned you in my easy-chair and bade you sit

Andante amoroso

still. I got my violin and tuned it down, because your piano is a little below concert pitch, and then we began. I played the "Hungarian Dances" because you like the swing and dash and color—you are a barbarian in some ways, dear—and then the softer, sweeter things.

Muting the strings, I played the "Legende" for you. I remember you said once that a muted violin sounded like a lover's voice and I wanted to tell you that it sounded as a lover felt.

When we played the "Serenade," I could see your white fingers on the keys. You seemed tired when we finished it, so we went over to the fire and sat down.

And then, just as I drew my chair up beside yours, I lost you! I could see you nowhere, and I looked around ruefully. In the midst of my despair, I saw you laughing at me from the fire. Little, mischievous sprite, how elusive you are!

There is a slender shaft of pussy willow in a bottle of water on my table. Last spring you picked it and laughingly gave it to me to keep. I planted it, and during the summer it grew into quite a tree. I brought a branch of it to my room a week ago, and to-night the tiny grey pussies have peeped out of their brown cover-lids. I don't wonder they call them pussy willows—they look like little Maltese paws when the claws are softly sheathed. I have deceived them shamefully with my fire, and they think it is spring.

The delicate, wholesome fragrance which clings to them makes me think of you, as what beautiful thing does not? I close my eyes and put my face down to them, and behold! it is spring, and I am standing in the woods with you. It is a kindlier power than Aladdin's lamp, for his talisman brought him nothing but gold, while mine, with unfailing tenderness, brings me the vision of you.

Easter

Largo

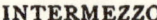

INTERMEZZO

MASCAGNI

raseggiando.

Easter

SUNDAY again, and I went to church this morning. For the simple reason, my Lady, that I was to help with the Easter music. Organ, harp, and violin played the Intermezzo and other things beautiful and appropriate, and I played the obligato for the contralto solo.

I never knew before what the Easter festival meant. I had thought it a time for fashion and show, but I passed by that this morning and grasped a deeper significance. I wish you could have seen the church, for vines swung and flowers bloomed everywhere. The chancel was a mass of Easter lilies, as sweet and as spotless as you.

The organ and the stained-glass windows, the vested choir and the lilies, appealed to me strongly. The bishop stood among the flowers with hands outstretched in blessing, and a shaft of golden light from the window struck full upon his face. It was a moment of consecration, of uplifting, of resurrection.

For my own part, the violin played of itself—I seemed to have no control whatever of the strings. Mascagni will never be forgotten because of his Intermezzo, and I know it so well I could play it with my eyes shut.

And as I played, a weight seemed lifted from my heart. The dull, dead pain that settled down upon me when I lost you for all time, was mercifully eased. It seemed as if you must be in the church, but I knew you were not, for there was no face there so flower-like and dear as yours.

I half expected it would come again, but it has not. There is a reaction after every pain —a sort of blessed calm that is almost Paradise. I felt my littleness, my selfishness.

We consider things so wholly from our own point of view ! My heart ached bitterly because I could not have you, and now it sings because I know you and love you.

Why, dear Lady, think of the countless people who have never seen you and never will ! And I, blessed above my fellows, have been your friend and you are still mine. More than this, there is no other to whom you are as dear and close as you are to me. I do not believe that any other man sees you in every flower and hears you in all the music that sings inside and outside his heart. And no one else writes to you as I do and directs and stamps the letters, and posts them—in his trunk. You are not lost — my loving you makes you mine.

Something of this came to me then and I have analysed it since. I do not know where it came from, whether in the beam of light that came through the window, in the heart of some one of those lilies that made me think of you, or on the soft wings of the Intermezzo, but it came, and I know now what resurrection may mean, for there is an Easter in my soul.

Buried Music

Largo

LEGENDE   WIENIAWSKI

54

Buried Music

THERE is a sweetness in the air to-day, and
I have opened my window. It blew in
upon me while I worked and is moving the
paper to-night, while I write to you. I am
going to the country soon, and three days in
the week I shall come in to my studio, but the
rest of the time I shall wander through the
fields and woods, compose a little, and think
much more of you.

Adelaide means very little to us, who have
the music of Beethoven, but ah, how much
she meant to him! More, perhaps, than his
music means to us. I am wondering if I shall
ever compose anything that shall mean as
much to the world as you do to me. If I do
—but no; neither opera nor symphony could
be great enough to hold that.

My work is neglected to-night. I should
be preparing for a concert next week and
writing out an obligato to a song that has

Largo

been sent to me, and see what I am doing instead!

It seems strange to think that my violin was once a tree, but I do not know what else could have caught the music that lies within it, waiting for the touch. It must be centuries old, and through all those years it was listening and learning, weaving in with its growth the forest melodies to sing to generations yet unborn.

Wind and wave and song of bird, crash of thunder, drip of rain, and mating-call—all these are in the fibre of my violin. And the thousand notes of sea and storm, the music of the waterfall and stream—what wonder that it is so nearly the human voice! There must have been a love story in that forest, for it sings love, love, and only love, though I do not remember of hearing it until I knew you.

Perhaps you have taught it a new melody —stranger things have happened—and it has learned your lesson best.

All the rest of its days it shall sing your song and perhaps some heart may learn its comforting. I am happy to-night, happier than I have ever been in my life, for the pain has not come back and I have only the joy of my loving without its grief.

Perhaps it is the swiftly coming spring, for all the world is new, and why should not hearts beat stronger now? There is no outward sign of it yet, except tiny tips of green that are hardly more than a promise, but I know, for this morning, just at dawn, I saw a flock of wild geese making their way northward through the cold grey of the sky.

What faith must carry them onward! I watched them as long as I could see, flying in their straight, precise lines, and as I looked, the leader grew tired of breasting the cold wind for the rest and dropped back, while, without pausing, another took his place.

I mean no more to the world than any one of that steady, patient flock, and yet if I do not falter, some single heart may look up, in simple reverence, to my faith and unfaltering.

PART TWO

59

April's Lady

Allegro

SPRING SONG

MENDELSSOHN

62

April's Lady

MY first day in the country has been that blending of sun and cloud which unfailingly marks the caprice and tenderness of April. The morning began beautifully, but in an hour the sky was grey and cheerless, and then we had a shower. It beat upon the windows like some mischievous sprite making a holiday, and I could almost see the little genius of the rain as I sat watching it.

Long silver shafts of water seemed almost to pierce the panes, and the swirl of it took form and became a teasing fairy, weaving a misty spell. I could see her at the window, in a robe that changed from grey to silver, sending arrows of rain from a cloudy quiver and laughing at me through the shimmering veil of her hair. The sun came out and the rain sprite flew away, doubtless to make mischief elsewhere.

Outside, every single sceptre of grass had

Allegro

its diamond drop at the end of it. The leaves were turning happy faces toward the sun, and the air was sweet with the freshness which comes only when wilful April asks pardon for her petulance.

All day the sky has been undecided between sun and shadow. Sometimes it has been grey and foreboding, then almost instantly bright again. Is there any blue, I wonder, like that of an April sky?

This afternoon, out of a seemingly pleasant heaven, we had another shower — a burst of tears with smiles in it. Lady April was laughing in spite of her weeping, for the sun was shining all through the rain.

I stood on the steps of my little house and watched it, for who would go indoors when the sun was shining! The drops of rain rushed sparkling through the air, and through every one of them shot a javelin of light. There were rainbows everywhere—hanging from the trees like some elfin drapery, poised in the air like a bird on the wing, and lying on the grass like children tired of their play.

The shower ceased and a pair of flame-coloured wings came down from unknown heights with a dazzling swiftness. His Majesty, Sir Oriole, perched on the topmost point of my tallest evergreen and opened his golden throat in such a flood of song that I no longer wondered where Mendelssohn learned - his melody of the spring. He was alive with the joy of living and sang because he must. He plumed his breast for a final cadenza, and while he was quivering with the ecstasy of it, the faithless evergreen bough tottered and broke. With a disappointed little chirp at the interruption, my sunset singer flew off to some kindlier foothold.

I have been thinking since that Sir Oriole must be in love, for nothing else could fill him with the rapture that was his. May he have a prosperous wooing !

Spring is a hint, a suggestion of the summer that is to come. Since the shades were drawn and the lamps lighted, I have been playing the Spring Song and trying to catch the beauty there is in it. It is almost too delicate for anything but a violin, unless some silver flute could capture the ripple and rush of it.

In moods like this, I am on the verge of composition, but I cannot write what I feel, save in these letters to you. Two little lines have been singing themselves over all day :

If you were April's Lady,
And I were Lord of May.

That is just what you are, my Heart, "April's Lady." You are as sunny and capricious as to-day has been, with your gleams of tenderness and your playful pouting, your laughing, childish cruelty, and your rainbow moods. Long as I have known you, I find you as far from me as ever. Some men boast that they know women, but I have never heard anyone make claim to knowing you.

In April there is a hint of the heart of summer and I am wondering if some fortunate June may find a heart in you. I almost hope that he may not, for I want no thorns showing themselves among your roses.

But since I have not the summer, I am thankful for the spring, and like some thirsty sparrow, exulting in an April shower, I can look up through the rain and be glad.

A Mating-Call

Allegro vivace

The rob - in sings in the ap - ple tree,

A Mating-Call

I FOUND the first violet to-day, half hidden under the leaves of autumn, wet with yesterday's rain.   It was such a pale, timid, shivering thing !   I covered it up with some dry leaves, and I hope it may be content to wait a little while longer before blossoming again.

Allegro vivace

These first impatient violets make me think of children and their Christmas stockings. After lying awake most of the night, listening for the bells of the reindeer, they creep out while it is still dark to claim their treasures. They find queer, knobby packages, but cannot tell their contents until daylight, and lie there, eating candy and watching with strained expectancy for the first gleam of dawn through the shutter.

The foolish little flowers know that spring is coming, but they are not content to wait until they feel the warmth through their brown coverlids.   They must needs put out

A
Mating
Call

their curious heads as soon as they wake, and instead of the beautiful spring of which they have heard so much, they find a cold, bare world, which treats them unkindly, and die, firmly believing that old Mother Nature has told them an untruth.

I have been watching a courtship to-day in the boughs of the apple tree just outside my window. Master Robin has been so absorbed in his wooing that he had no time to notice me. The lady of his choice sat on the branch above him, fully aware of my presence, for it is always the woman who has a care for outsiders.

She has been cold and aloof; apparently his pleadings and protestations have not concerned her in the least, but I could see the twinkle in her eyes when she turned her head away from him.

Her Robin has proved himself a valiant lover, for he has been under her leafy casement this entire day, saving short intervals for refreshment. Once, seeing that she had no respect for words, he determined to win her with gifts, and flew away, without a word of farewell, in search of some bid for her favour.

My Lady Robin was plainly nervous and unhappy when he left her, yet she was too proud to let me see her agitation. She glanced around unconcernedly, and plumed herself with an air of aristocratic indifference. It takes birds and women a long time to learn that the true lover will always come back.

When he returned with a fat worm in his beak, she started with joy, but was too wary to let him see her pleasure, and proudly disdained the proffered worm. After vain pleading, he ate it himself with evident satisfaction, and settled down to go over the argument again.

Such chirping and twittering and singing ! He was plainly describing the kind of house he intended to build for her, for she turned a scornful look on him as he ·hopped from bough to bough, evidently illustrating the ground plan of it.

Then, throwing aside worldly considerations, he sang the old love-song, the first the world heard, and the last it will hear, filling it with such an indescribable wealth of feeling that his love's eyes shone with happy pride. I could see that she was won, but her blind adorer puffed out his scarlet breast and sang with such passionate beauty that she could not say a word. At last, just at sunset, she went over to him, with a shy, coquettish twist of her head, a sparkle in her eyes, and a single, half-whispered chirp that I could understand as well as he. I shall never forget the exultant poise of wing with which he soared aloft, with her beside him. Wing and wing together, they sailed westward toward the sunset, until they were lost in the crimson glow.

Seeing all the world making a wedding-day, do you wonder at my loneliness? Ah, Sweetheart, if song could win a woman, I would take my stand under your window with my violin, and play until your heart turned to mine.

But I would want no heavenly flight, even toward the gold of sunset, for this earth is heaven enough when the light of love shines upon it, and rather than wing and wing through the sweet, cool air, I would go down leafy lanes blossoming with violets, hand in hand with you.

The Dawn of May

Andante

The Dawn of May

TO-DAY I have had a long walk through the woods and fields. The Earth has thrown off her lethargy and waked into living. Everything is budded now, and soon will come the time of blossoming.

The hepaticas and windflowers, rash children of the woods that they are, have already made little pink and white spots of beauty among the brown, dead leaves. There is a tender flush on Nature's withered face, that means rebirth and resurrection.

On the southern slope of a hill I found a yellow violet. There seems to be a passion this year for early rising. The trilliums, brave and bonny in their new attire, are too proud to speak to the passer-by. I bent down to one of them, but not a glance could I get.

Jack-in-the-Pulpit was turning tender eyes that way. He stood, well-dressed and haughty, close beside Mistress Trillium, who leaned towards him with an air of delicate encouragement. Perhaps that is why she had no inclination to look at me.

The plain of woods just east of the maple grove seems like a vast festival. The guests are brilliant and stately, only moving aside gracefully when some gay wind goes by. The hepaticas are gowned in white just touched with a delicate pink, the windflowers are clothed with a warmer shade, and the violets, in their ever varying purple, almost monopolise the field.

The air is full of meaning. One feels that something great is about to happen, whether it be some ceremonial procession, in which all the guests are to join, swinging their perfumed censers and chanting the ever joyous hymn of spring, or whether some sweet fairy symphony is to be played on hidden strings, too far off and faint for our human ears to hear.

I think they miss you, Sweetheart, unless your passing this way once is joy enough for one field. You have been beside me all day, singing softly to yourself as you have always done in the woods, and every now and then turning your face, fairer and sweeter than any flower that grows, up to mine.

There are no depths in any stream like the brown, soft tenderness of your eyes, no melody in wind or wave like the ever-changing music of your voice, and no sweetness in all the world is like that within the scarlet chalice of your lips.

I wonder what the flowers do when the stars come out! Do they wait, half-shyly half-fearfully, for the dawn? Perhaps they cuddle down closer among their leaves and listen to the slumbrous voices of the night.

I open my window a tiny crack when the spring nights come, and put my violin against the casement, and listen. The delicate fingers of May pick out melodies upon those strings, such as Mozart never sang. Faint, far-off, and tender, like some half-hushed lullaby, I have heard a dream-song to-night that the wind never played before.

I have taken my violin away now and opened the window wide. And then, because I know it will never reach you and because it comforts my heart to give it, I send a kiss across the sleeping world to where my Lady sleeps.

The Trumpeters

Larghetto

79

The Trumpeters

Larghetto

THE East Wind brought a sweet, far-off odour to-day, and I started out in search of it. I knew what it was—the wild phlox.

I found it in a little hollow near the river, a whole plain of it, filling the air with that subtle fragrance that no one ever forgets. The yellow buttercups had a part of the place to themselves, making a wilderness of gold and blue. I sat down among them, where I could see the river and the sky.

What a stately trumpeter the wild phlox is! There was a single shaft of it near me, rugged and yet graceful, gay with its martial blue. It stood straight as a soldier might, with his long blue trumpet to his lips, marshalling the fields in proud array with his triumphant bugle-call. What army does he lead? What elfin music does he play? All the little people of the forest know, but we cannot hear and they cannot tell.

And yet they follow him. The hepaticas
and violets are his advance-guard and the
army comes behind. Rows upon rows of
buttercups, flaunting the cavalry yellow, ride
in his train, and then come tired troops of
humbler soldiers, caring little for trumpet and
drum, and following as best they may.

The passing of the army leaves desolation
behind. Some soldiers die on the way, and
the rest go on, as the children followed the
Pied Piper into the mountain side. We may
call and call, but they never come back, and
the next year the Blue Trumpeter calls again,
and the flower soldiers, with never a sigh,
join the vanishing train.

We cannot hear the martial music to which
their feet keep time ; we have no hint of the
far-off land to which their troops go forth.
They never return, and each year another
army springs up, only to be led away.

Perhaps they journey to some distant bourne
where it is always spring, to some country
whose margin the snows of winter never
reach, and where the icy blasts are mellowed
to a gentle summer wind.

There must be some place for human hearts

in a land like that, some balm for human pain. We follow the White Trumpeter less willingly, for we know not of the country to which he leads us, and have no vision of those who dwell therein. But if the violets and buttercups go first, should we not be glad to follow?

Some day the White Trumpeter will summon me from sleep and I shall go willingly. But I shall beg him, ere I depart, to touch your eyelids too, not that I may see you and speak to you, but because no land could be dark or dreary where you should bide.

There is no return from that far-off country, so I would not have you led thither till you were aweary of this ; but no cloud of sorrow could reach me there if I knew you were one day coming, for you would glorify a desert place for me, even if I might only look upon the paths where once your feet had trod.

Sunset on the Marsh

Adagio appassionato

SEELING

86

Sunset on the Marsh

THE marsh is gay with blue flags that stream in every wind. I have been down to the bank of it, watching the birds skim lightly over its surface and looking through the tall grasses to the opposite edge of it.

It is so still down there ! Nothing but the nodding, sleepy sway of the grasses and the cry of the bobolink, the turquoise-blue sky overhead, and the wide stretch of plain.

I got my little boat and pushed out into the tiny stream that runs into the marsh. There was scarcely water enough to float it, and the grasses reached almost to my head. One might so easily be lost there !

Sitting among them, with the yellow marsh lilies and the tall iris so near that I could almost reach them, I began to think of you. There is nothing, since the day I saw you first, that is not embalmed in the amber of my memory. Not a mood of yours is lost.

Adagio appassionato

You had no idea, my Lady, of the watch that was kept over you, and I do not think you can know now. There is no recollection like that of loving, for love itself is recollection, and in loving one loves all the thousand memories that store themselves away.

I have wondered vainly many times why I love you and tried to pick out this quality and that for my especial regard. This afternoon, in the marsh, I found out. It is your crystalline, exquisite honour.

The purity of most women is negative; they are clean because they are not otherwise. Yours is positive—you are white because God made you so, and mingled with this is a holy joy in your whiteness. I felt, the first time I saw you, as if I should stand in your presence with uncovered head, and I never knew why until this afternoon.

How long I sat there I shall never know, but I awoke with a start, and looking over the field of blue flags, saw the sunset.

It was a divine moment and I felt as Sidney Lanier must have felt when he wrote, in his *Sunrise on the Marshes :*

Oh, what if a sound should be made !
Oh, what if a hand should be laid
On this bow- and string-tension of beauty and silence
  a-spring,—

The tall, nodding plumes of grass and iris were touched with an exquisite light ; the circling swallows were hovering on silent, expectant wing, and the pools of water were blood-red. I began to push out, keeping my face fixed upon the western sky, and the splash of the paddle in the water seemed almost too much to be borne.

I stopped at the entrance to the little river and my boat swung out into that sunset glow. The air was opalescent and shimmering, and with a sudden flash of light the pools became gold where they had been blood-red. There was a burst of flame that would be music to finer ears than ours, and then the marsh trembled into shadow, then into twilight, and finally dark.

The Lost Path

Andante amoroso

TRAUMEREI

The Lost Path

L AST night, while all the world slumbered and slept, there was a miracle. It had been going on for months, silently, in tiny hidden chambers, and this morning saw the fulfilment.

My Lady, this part of the earth is radiant with pink and white blossoming. The boughs of the trees seem to bend beneath their weight of fragrant snow. And there is not one blossom among them worthy to be compared with your face.

What a strange chemistry goes on within those dark, winding passages ! There must be a mighty quiver of life in that mysterious labyrinth to break forth into such beauty as this.

To-night the South Wind, warm and sweet, is blowing through the fields. It comes through my open door and carries with it the breath of the orchard.

Andante amoroso

The Wind is a gay gallant and more fickle than either man or woman has dared to be. It has ruffled the surface of a thousand streams and then gone on. All the time it croons that soft, low, dreamy song that startles the flowers and thrills the plains with joy.

Over fields of daisies it has come, laughing and singing, and setting every bluebell in the south to ringing merrily. Now it has left the apple blossoms in mourning, and is moving my paper as I write, and, yes, singing to me of you.

All things sing of you, Dear Heart. I hear your name in every wind that blows and see your face in every flower. I cannot wholly lose you, even though you have denied yourself to me.

I wonder if you would be willing to go back, not knowing that I love you, and live our happy companionship over again ! I remember last summer, out in the woods, we found a little path that wandered bravely for a space, then hesitated and tried to turn, and was finally lost among the trees. You laughed and said : "See the poor little lost path!" And now I have one of my own.

Would you go back to those dear days in the woods and fields ? Or is your life already so full that you have forgotten me ? I made a large part of it then and now I am little, if anything, to you.

The memory of those days in the sweet, green, translucent forest comes back to-night, not wholly without pain. I see your face, full of pity for the poor lost path—surely you must have some for me.

Would you go back and live it all over again ? "I would turn back with you, Sweetheart,—yes, from the gate of Paradise."

The Garden of Years

Larghetto

WARUM

SCHUMANN

The Garden of Years

IN the Country of Time there is an old-fashioned Garden of Years, and therein each one of us has a little space in which we toil from the dawn of life to its close. We plant Hope and there springs up Despair, and many things we thought would comfort us with bloom and fragrance only sting and burn.

My garden is not completed yet and sometimes I fear that I shall leave my task half finished, but I work on as best I may, hoping that at the last the Wise Gardener may forgive mistakes and only take heed of the blossoms.

I was only a child when I found it, and to me it was a fairyland. I played all day with the bees and birds and filled my hands with flowers. But one day there came a change. I suddenly woke to the knowledge that it was mine, that my hands must sow and reap, and as the planting, so should the harvest be.

Larghetto

It was hard at first and I often grew weary and faint. But not until my planting went astray did I cry out in grief. I wanted only beauty and fragrance and there came up thorns. I made the paths smooth and even and in the morning they were overgrown with weeds and brambles.

Alien hands interfered with my sowing and dropped strange seeds in the ground. The weeds thrived and the flowers died, and where I planted heartsease there came up a nettle.

I took courage when I found that other gardens were the same as mine. There is one I know wherein a faithful soul has worked bravely and patiently much longer than I have. He was making the garden ready for an invited guest and the Angel of Sorrow came instead. He had planted his heart's blood, dreaming that Love would grow, and in place of it God's roses bloomed.

But in spite of the weeds and thorns, there is one spot of beauty in my garden that fills me with joy. When I am faint, I turn toward it and the sight refreshes me.

It is only a single flower, but the weeds do

not grow around it, and it is always in bloom. It is a tall, stately lily, white and sweet and fair, and so divinely fragrant that it comforts my tired soul. No alien fingers have marred the beauty of it ; no strange seeds have taken root in that soil. There is no disappointment so deep that the breath of that lily is not balm.

Do you know what it is, my Heart ? That single, stately, perfect blossom, for whose sake the Gardener will forgive all that is wrong, is my love for you.

The Army of the Clover

Allegro vivace

TERESITA WALTZ

CARREÑO

104

The Army of the Clover

SOMETHING is always happening down in the orchard. I went there two or three days ago and saw nothing unusual. The grass was green and soft and the apple blossoms were quiet and demure. But a strange army has invaded my country and encamped boldly in my domain.

All through the grass are the green tents of the clover. The saucy soldiers look up at me with serene impudence, vouchsafing only a hurried greeting. One would think I was the intruder!

They have stationed their picket-lines from one end of the orchard to the other. Here and there a scarlet captain, almost bursting with pride in his new uniform, keeps a gruff look-out for the enemy.

The pink-and-white infantry has not seen much service but is waging a defensive combat. The opposing army is beating

Allegro vivace

against their citadel and capturing their stores.

I saw one of the enemy's generals to-day in a fierce conflict with a gorgeous clover captain. His trousers were black and yellow and his weapon a bayonet. I fear the Army of the Clover stands small chance of winning the battle with the bees !

But in the matter of hearts, the army is supreme. The tiny soldiers have encamped wisely at the foot of the apple trees. Day by day they turn their faces upward in humble pleading for a word or a glance from the sweet ladies on the boughs.

There is a subtle difference in the Apple Blossom damsels. They are inclined to rustle their skirts with importance, but there is a telltale flush on more than one fair cheek which tells me that surrender is only a question of time.

A few have already gone over to the enemy, and a gallant enemy it is. A sturdy brigadier has kept a loving vigil under a leafy window with his eager eyes on one particular blossom. She is so sweet and white and fair I do not wonder at his choice.

My Lady Apple Blossom has been coy, but the patient arms have been outspread, waiting for her. She gave in at last and dropped, slowly and yet decidedly, close beside him. And others will follow.

Every wind that blows brings a shower of bloom from the trees, and the waiting army below rejoices. I notice that only the more mature ladies have been won as yet—the youngest of the Apple Blossoms are waiting. Some will wait a long time, for they are the merest children, tiny and helpless, in long white robes and wee pink hoods.

I suppose it is natural for the ladies to declare that it was the fault of the wind. Yet I have seen more than one, poised on ready wing, only waiting for the slightest breeze as an excuse. And I think the Clover Privates know, for I have seen more than one smile and turn his head aside when the lady of his heart heaped feminine invective upon "that horrid wind."

The gentlemen among the Apple Blossoms are resenting the Fabian warfare which results, strangely enough, in the loss of their fairest Sabines. And in their leisure moments, they are taking care of the children, for more than one baby Apple Blossom has been left to the awkward care of its father, while its mother has gone in the train of the Clover Army, preferring the melody of the pink trumpets to the inarticulate fragrance of her own children.

Dear Lady of my Heart, if you were an Apple Blossom and I a Clover Private, I would wait until one of us died before I would give you up, and all through the waiting I should pray for some kindly wind to blow you into my outstretched arms.

PART THREE

109

The River of Rest

Adagio appassionato

111

SLUMBER SONG

The River of Rest

Adagio appassionato

SUMMER has stolen upon us with her soft, dreamy wings, and the world is singing her praises. With a ripple of leaves and a tinkle of streams, the full earth rolls in a stately march, from sun to shadow and back to sun again.

There is a drowsy murmur of bells to-night, and looking across the fields, I can see the sheep going home. I have lulled myself to sleep many a time, fancying I saw them going one by one over the hill, and to-night, in the violet shadow, I see a picture so like that of my dreams that my eyelids droop even at the memory of it.

He was a brave man who first closed his eyes in sleep, but what a reward was his !

Within the borders of Slumberland lies the Country of Dreams, beyond the night and far, far past the day. The breath of a thousand springs is in the air and shadowy wings sweep over the fields, aflame with blossoms that only dreamers know.

There is a river winding through that country—they call it the River of Rest. The still, wide waters are cool and clear, and there is no room for disappointment on that lily-lined shore.

The sky is always blue there, and there is no heartache in my dream. You put your hand in mine and we go on together, through meadows brave with bloom.

The dead, lost violets of my happy days with you blossom afresh in those fair plains, and I watch the light in your eyes, forgetting the cruel gulf of years that must ever lie between your heart and mine.

Dear Lady, those fields are sweet with summer now, and you go on, without knowing how I love you. But it is only a step to the land where my hungry lips can speak to you and my empty hands grasp yours, and when I wake, I can only pray that I may dream again.

The hill over which the sheep have passed is lost in the shadow now, but I can hear the far-off tinkle which means "follow." Some mystic bell is calling me to that dear land where I always find you, and I shall obey, though I must pass through dark to reach it.

On the stately, majestic river there is a shallop moored among the lilies for me, and I shall find you there, with love on your face and the gold of sunset lying on your hair. We shall sail down the river together, dear Heart, and you will be a willing guest

In fancy I can see you now, as you reach over the side of the boat and trail your fingers in the water, half expecting to find them stained crimson with the reflected clouds. Then you will look up at me, smiling, and point toward the west, where, upraised on a slender pillar of purple cloud, is the faint, exquisite lamp of a star.

Roses

Allegro

TO A WILD ROSE

Roses

Allegro

IS there anything in the world like a rose?
The earth is glorious with them to-night
and that means June. Beneath my window a
stately bush flaunts a wealth of yellow blossoms that make a luminous, sweet place, even
in the dark. It might be some fair Atalanta,
flying from the wind with her golden hair
streaming like a veil behind her.

My garden is carefully tended, but there is
a wilder, dearer one on every roadside. There
no man has planted and no man tills, but
masses of pink-and-white bloom are drifted
like sunrise clouds. I have been among them
all day, the thorny, sweet wild roses, with
all the fragrance of their garden sisters and
none of their pretensions.

With some of them it is a time of penance
and prayer. They are humbled in the dust of
the roadside, their heads bowed in shame.
Others, less conscientious, have doffed their

"winter garment of repentance," and dance in stately fashion with every passing breeze.

Among the penitents are some in priestly garb, white and spotless, swinging perfumed censers. They seem to be ministers of grace to all the roses in the field. One of them is particularly austere and forbidding. He evidently frowns on all gayety, for he has only one pensioner for his pardon—a flushed, tearful wild rose, who kneels at his feet in a guilty confessional.

For what sin does she crave absolution ! There can be only one; that of open, wilful coquetry. Sir South Wind has found his fate at last and he will retire broken-hearted from the contest with Mistress Rose.

There is a yellow rose suffering social ostracism on account of its colour. It is as fair and sweet as any of the others, but because pink is the prevailing fashion it must needs be cast aside. Weeping, it sits alone in a dusty, deserted place, drooping and dejected. There is need for the priestly comfort here, but there is no heaven for yellow roses; only for pink and white.

To-morrow I shall transplant it to my garden, at the foot of the brave, bonny Atalanta beneath my window. I wish there were some way of making the pink roses understand that it had gone to a better place.

There is no colour among them that is not copied from the sky, and it seems as if some spirit of light must come from the clouds, with a palette of sunrise tints, to paint each separate rose a different shade. I think I saw the fairy artist at his work this morning, for just at dawn I went out to the wild-rose garden, walking softly lest I should disturb their sleep, and close by the roadside I heard a gentle rustle of leaves.

I looked down, and in the first beam of light from the rising sun there was a shimmer of gossamer wings and just a flash of rainbow in the dewy mist above the grass.

Children of the Air

Andante

123

Children of the Air

A FAIRY frigate floated by my window to-day, bound for some port on the airy sea. The Thistledown fleet has not cast off its anchor yet and this was doubtless a special envoy on some important mission.

In spite of its elusiveness, I captured it and set it free, a winged kiss, to find your cheek. If you loved me, dear, I think you would know, the moment the downy messenger came near you, of the freight it held for you.

What compass sets the tiny ships of air toward their destined harbour ! They seem to be the sport of every wind that blows, and yet they steadfastly sail toward the blue, distant haven that is to mark the end of their journeying. They are turned aside, but not diverted, by untoward fate.

I know the precious cargo that lies within the hold—a baby thistle, cradled in softest down. Within that tiny speck is a germ of

life, marvellously potent, that next summer
will blossom into a royal thistle, stern and
haughty in his thorny, purple majesty.

And so, within a softer shrine than any
Thistledown has dared to dream of, lies the
precious jewel of your heart, that has blos-
somed into a woman.

The air is full of messages to-day and the
winged postmen are going back and forth on
some momentous errand. Some are gorgeous
in black and scarlet livery, as if a red rose
had tried to masquerade in the sable of the
night, that none might know she had taken
wing.

From the countless yellow butterflies that
have been sweeping over the fields to-day, I
think the golden roses must have determined
to leave in a body. There are only a few left
—all the rest are on their airy journey.

Even with the coming of night the busy
messengers have not ceased to travel. Outside there are tiny flashes of flame that
sparkle for a moment and then disappear.

Perhaps the Thistledown envoys have taken
a crimson flagship for their guide through
unknown waters, or perhaps the butterflies

have found some way of preserving sunlight
for use at night.

I have charged every one of them with a kiss for you. Some of them will find you, doubtless, but you will not know what it is that touches your brow so softly. You will brush away the impertinent thistledown and feel aggrieved at the butterflies, and I know that the tiny lamp-bearers will never get within arm's length of you, but it will be strange if among them they do not make you think once, and perhaps not unkindly, of me.

A Woman's Hand

Larghetto

CONSOLATION

MENDELSSOHN

A Woman's Hand

THE morning-glories outside my window greet me with a smile every day. There is one particular blossom, white and delicately veined, with just a flush of rose at the edge, that makes me think of your hand.

No man ever reached the heights unless he felt the touch of some good woman's fingers, and no man's life has been strong unless he knew of that sweet sculpturing.

From the day of his birth to the gate of his grave, that hand is his ministering angel. It soothes his childish fretting and closes his eyes in his last slumber. When he is in despair, it bids him take heart again, and when his body is racked with pain, it lies with soft coolness on his fevered face and charms the pain away.

It unlocks the door of glory and bids him win those honors of which fame keeps the key. It reaches out across the dark to touch

Larghetto

him with gentle consolation and it always thrills him with its sweet tenderness. Holding to that offered hand, man has climbed from the depths step by step, blessing the gracious womanliness that offered it.

Upon my life there lies the print of a woman's palm, rosy, soft, and tender—ah, my Heart, you know whose hand it is ! Day by day I have felt it, continually leading me upward, smoothing down the roughness in my nature, and teaching me to live. As much as I am more than I might have been, I owe to that kindly hand.

The knowledge has been comforting more than once, that only by walking a little way I might hold it in my own for an instant, wondering at the softness of it and gaining strength from its power.

And now, just because you know that I love you better than all the world beside, I can never touch your hand again, never feel your palm against mine, never reach out in sorrow or discouragement, to learn its message of cheer.

It is a strange decree of Fate that when a man loves a woman he must give up everything he has of hers, if she cannot give him all. I wonder if they think Love ever forgets!

But though I cannot see you nor have even a word from you, I am happy because I can love you and in fancy have you daily by my side. And I do not need to touch your hand to know all its gentle tenderness, for just by thinking of you I can feel it, warm and soft, within my own.

The memory of it shall keep me from despair, and all my life I shall thank God that I have known the touch of it once, to lead me to the heights I could never reach without it and to replace my doubt and unbelief with a simple, reverent trust.

A Dream-Ship

Larghetto

VENETIAN BOAT SONG

MENDELSSOHN

136

A Dream=Ship

LAST night I dreamed that I stood on the sea shore, watching the leaning sails of my ship sailing forth in search of gold. Her new colors flew bravely at the masthead and I looked until I could see no longer. When I turned back, you stood beside me, your eyes alight with love, and I put you away. I said: "Wait till the ship comes back—then there will be gold."

I watched in the shadow with silent eagerness, but no sail came above the horizon. Somewhere, out on that measureless blue meadow, all my hopes were drifting. You held out your arms to me and said : "Why wait for the ship to come back ? It is I you need, not gold."

I put you away again, and you went on down the sand with a pathetic droop in your shoulders. I was going to follow you, but just then I saw a sail. It shone whitely

Largbetto

against the sunrise after the long, dark night, and I called to you to come back, but you went on and on. Call as I might, you did not hear. I knew there were gold and jewels and silks and spices for you, but you wanted none of them.

I looked back to the sea and it was grey. The waters, remembering, beat cold on the shore. I listened in vain for your pleading voice, and the ship came nearer and nearer, laden with spices and gold.

The sea birds cried hoarsely, thronging over the masthead and flying round the streaming colors, but I had no eyes for the approaching treasure. Deep down in my soul throbbed a bitter, stinging pain. I had lost you ; but my ship was coming in.

Dear Lady of my Heart, I never awoke from a dream so gladly as from that. To think that you should hold out your arms to me and I should turn away ! I have held out mine to you and you have turned aside, but that was your privilege.

I see, of course, that you can never love me, but it seems as if you must.

I struck my tuning-fork near my violin to-

day, and the string vibrated in reply, I tried
it with the piano and the result was the same.
I have sounded a single string on my violin
near an organ pipe of the same tone, and the
dark, hollow shaft took up the note in answer.
So why should not my love for you awake at
least an echo in your heart?

If it could be given me to hear the faintest
responding tone, I think that single, half-
hushed note would swell through my soul
like the resonant majesty of a symphony.

The Moth and the Star

Doloroso

FUNERAL MARCH

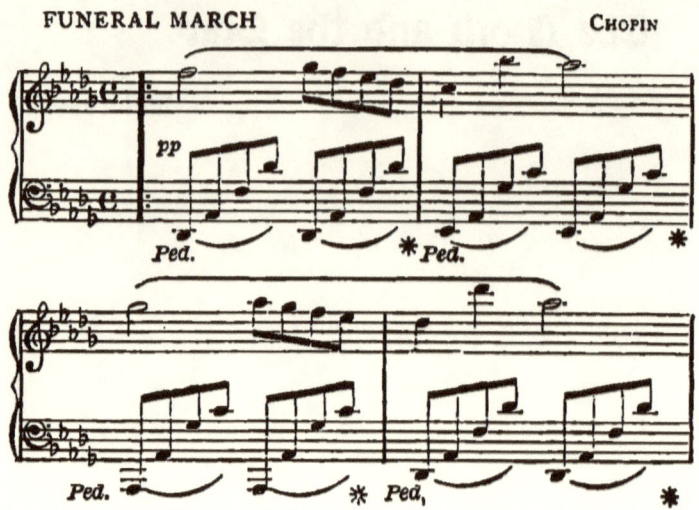

The Moth and the Star

THE fields are green with new life. The inward heart of the wheat is throbbing with a thousand pulses that mean a harvest by and by.

Each single spire of green reaches down into the ground and draws up the food it needs, making it into spear and blossom. I have been wondering what goes on under the surface of the ground and if there is another life below.

Somewhere there must be a stairway, leading from the heat of summer down into those cool, dark chambers, through mysterious winding passages. The trees find strength and beauty down there, the wheat finds all its fibre and the flowers find their blossoms.

I can dream of nothing there for me except rest and I should surely find that. The blind rain would not beat coldly on me then, though my face should be turned upward to the grass, and the wind could not pierce me with its cold. No word of kindness could reach me there, but the harsh ones would go on by. The green leaves would murmur afresh every spring, and I should not hear their gentle music—no sound of earth would awaken me.

If you were lying there, I should find that stairway and descend. You would not know, but I would, for even in the earth beside you I should dream of loving you.

The wheat-fields are joyous to-day, but I am strangely sad. The birds sing, and my heart beats out only pain. My journey is so lonely that I am beginning to falter, even with the memory of you to comfort me. Eight months have passed, and the old, bitter grief has not lessened. I still flutter vainly, like a moth, around your candle-flame.

Will it ever change? I think of you constantly and it should mean happiness, but sometimes there comes a pain so deep and wide that my heart cries out with the bitterness of it.

You are far away from me—even in death I could not hope to reach you. It is the old story of the moth aspiring to the star. The light dazzles me and I forget and go too near, and, turning away with blinded eyes, I only see the dark.

I think the night cannot be far away, my Lady, when I shall turn away and sink, suffering, to the ground. But I shall not mind the pain of it so much, because I have seen the white beauty of the flame.

Awheel at Dawn

Allegro vivace

Awheel at Dawn

THAT first harbinger of autumn, the goldenrod, has taken possession of the fields
and roadways. I wheeled through aromatic
aisles of it this morning, just before sunrise.

Allegro
vivace

There is no joy like that—to follow the
wind at dawn, with a living, sparkling thing
of steel for a steed. You were beside me
this morning and the vision of you was so
real that I once or twice put out my hand to
touch you when we came to a steep hill.

You are a mischievous little witch about
hill-climbing. I have a suspicion that you regard a steep ascent as the keenest pleasure. I
know your feet are busy, but your eyes dance
with fun, and I notice that when I have your
hand in mine, I am invariably ahead. But I
rather like it, Sweetheart ; one would gladly
be any kind of a horse if the coach might
always hold so sweet an occupant.

Oh, the exultant thrill of life, when one can

be awheel in an autumn dawn ! Every muscle seems to sing in rapturous accord. If the birds find the same delight in flying, it is not strange that every sunrise is a chorus and every grove a temple of song.

Down on the goldenrod road is a company of purple asters, the first of the stately monarchs of the field that make the days of autumn a coronation. The nodding goldenrod woke this morning with a half-sleepy sigh, while the aster was still dreaming of the long, sweet days yet to come.

On I sped toward the wide gates of Eastern gold. Then there was a sheen of light on the handle-bar and I knew the day had begun. Out in the meadow, across the blowing clover, a meadow-lark soared aloft and sang as only a meadow-lark can sing, in greeting to the sun.

From out the silvery throat of that child of the morning came such a flood of melody that I stopped to listen. His breast was ashine with dew, his wings were thrilling with abounding, triumphant life. The wind came across the clover, bringing a shaft of light that touched my wheels with silver, and in that pæan of praise my heart joined too.

Flood Tide

Larghetto

BY THE SEA

Flood Tide

HARVEST is beginning and the tide of the year is at flood now. Every bud and blossom of spring and summer has attained the purpose of its life in fruit. The fields are golden and glorious and the world is radiant with beauty.

All day, with the hum of bees and the twittering of birds, comes the soft melody of reaping. Hay and clover have filled the air with their dying, fragrant breath, and now the wheat shall follow.

This time of year makes me think of Tennyson's death-bed. I do not believe even his poet fancy could have pictured a more beautiful ending to a life so rich with song.

I can look across the fields and fancy it is England, and that in a little room whose twilight stillness my eyes can penetrate, the Master lies in seeming sleep. He is stately in his repose and the light on his face seems to

Larghetto

Flood
Tide

come from within, rather than from without.

The harvest-fields below, where the grain is bound in sheaves, are mellowed by the sunset, then by the violet shadows of twilight, and then dark. But the harvest moon swings up, its slow light changing from red to gold.

> " Twilight and evening bell
> And after that—the dark—"

His own words, vibrant with meaning, strike with a new melody upon the ear. Twilight has passed, the echo of the evening bell has died away, and now comes the dark.

The moon rises higher and higher in the heavens and makes the little room as bright as day. The Master turns and asks for his Shakespeare. The old, worn volume, ever new, is put into his hands, and holding it, he repeats softly the dirge from "Cymbeline."

> " Fear no more the heat o' th' sun,
> Nor the furious winter's rages ;
> Thou thy worldly task hast done
> Home art gone, and ta'en thy wages."

Could there be a time so meet as harvest for his life to be gathered in ? There is no brighter sheaf in the field of immortals, saving only him whose words the dying Master repeated.

> " Fear no more the lightning flash
> Nor th' all dreaded thunder-stone ;
> Fear not slander, censure rash ;
> Thou hast finished joy and moan—"

With the last words of the dirge England's light went out, and in with her harvest went her tears.

With every wheat-field I have seen, has come that memory of the Laureate's last hour. He had wished to go out with the tide, with "no moaning of the bar," and "no sadness of farewell."

The tide of the year was swelling at flood when he joined it, and its recession took a greater gift than its flow had brought. But he took no reck of the world's loss, for he was face to face with his Pilot—"across the bar."

Two Harvest-Fields

Largo

157

Ruh'n in Frie - de   al - - le See - len.

Two Harvest=Fields

I HAVE been walking through the harvest-
fields to-night, and you have been beside
me, though you did not know. The harvest
moon was at full and its mellow light flooded
all the earth with gold. I grew faint with
longing to tell you all the love of which you
can never dream and of which words are too
weak to carry the meaning.

Heart-deep among the sheaves of ripened
wheat, I seemed to feel your dear arms cling-
ing. Undreamed-of tenderness was in your
eyes, and my soul sung in rapture such as
neither bird nor flute could reach. Then, you
let me touch your lips.

Half of the field has not been touched by
the reapers, and here the scarlet poppies were
drifting their brave bloom through the gold. If
the cup of slumber could give me the dream of
your arms and lips, I would drain it to its dregs
to-night and live always in your tenderness.

But I have nothing to look forward to, save

Largo

that other field I saw to-night, on the side of the hill.

There is a garnered treasure there and the winnowing is over. Stately shafts of bridal white keep solemn guard—they are the sentinels in God's harvest-field.

No poppies drift their riotous bloom on that hillside and no sound of reaping breaks the stillness. The songs are hushed and the singers pass that field in reverent silence because they cannot understand its harvest.

We never learn that mystery until after we have solved it, and after knowing, we cannot tell. Each must journey for himself to the country whose margin lies just beyond the bounds of our every-day life, and yet is as strange and as vast as the sea.

The poppies have no ministry there, for they who sleep in that country need no silken leaves to bring them rest.

Some day my harvest will be gathered in, small and scant as it is, but I know the Reaper will forgive its pathetic, broken store. And in whatever land you dwell, I want my face turned toward you, so that if there be dreaming in the dark, I may dream of you.

The Angel of the Darker Drink

Doloroso

MISERERE   VERDI

162

The Angel of the Darker Drink

IT has been almost a year since I saw your face, and every day now brings a shuddering pain. Yesterday and to-day I have not been able to see you in my fancy, to hear your voice, or to touch your hand. I cannot remember your eyes or lips or hair, and only a week ago I could at any moment find you by my side. I cannot write to you any longer and watch with a foolish fancy for your answer. Everything is mysteriously changed. I only know that I love you and have lost you —that even the vision of you is no longer mine.

You cannot imagine what a comfort it has been to have you always by my side. And now I have lost you and the world is cold. I cannot write it—I can only feel, and reach out vainly through my despair for something—I know not what.

I have been trying to compose, but I cannot

work. I had a sonata for violin and piano almost finished, and it was to be dedicated to you. I did not tell you before because I wanted to surprise you, and now I have lost you!

I cry out, "Come back! come back!" but you take no heed. My vision has forever left me and I am desolate and alone.

One of the quatrains in the "Rubaiyat" has been singing itself over and over—

" So when the Angel of the Darker Drink
   At last shall find you by the river-brink
      And, offering his Cup, invite your soul
   Forth to your lips to quaff—you shall not shrink."

If that gracious Angel were to offer his Cup to me, how gladly would I drink it! I would turn away from the black of this world without you, and bury my face in his grey, soft wings. No grave roof can be heavier than my despair. I have lost you—lost you—lost you!

The room seems to whirl and everything is growing black. I write these last few lines without being able to see the paper. It does not matter. I have lost you—lost you! It is dark—so dark——

.   .   .   .

A Wedding March

Jubilate

165

BRIDAL CHORUS

WAGNER

166

A Wedding March

DEAREST LADY :

JUST one more letter, which I am going to put into your own hands with the violets you said you would wear for me, even if you had to hide them under the laces of your gown.

If I had dreamed that the letters I posted in my trunk would eventually attain the dignity of a real letter-box, I should have taken better care of them. You would never have had them, anyway, if they had not found them while I was too ill to speak or to know what they were doing, but with all my soul I bless the hand that interfered.

I have no idea now of what I wrote, and you, with your sovereign right, have refused to let me have even a glimpse of my own pages. You say they are not mine, but yours, and you are right, for I am yours, and whatever I possess is yours, wholly and eternally.

Do you know what I thought, my Life, when I woke out of the delirium of fever and found you sitting beside me, with my hand in yours? I thought I had reached Heaven, and instead of rewarding me with a crown of righteousness, God had given me you. I was afraid to speak for fear you would vanish, and I had no idea you were real, until you leaned down with tears in your eyes and a flush on your cheek, and—no, I cannot write it, even to you.

The hours are passing on leaden feet this afternoon and it seems as if the evening will never come. But I know that it will, and that after all these weeks of confusion, I shall see you alone for one dear moment, in the shimmering white of your wedding gown. And if you will let me, I shall pin the violets over the truest heart in the world, and ask them to tell you better than I can do, of the wealth of love that is yours.

You must know it, even if my words are too weak to tell you, for nothing but your belief in it and a little of it in your own heart could have made you come to me as you did.

In fancy I can hear the organ now, pealing

out the sonorous chords of the wedding march from Lohengrin. There is nothing else in the world that could possibly do. Had I the gift, I should write one, but no organ has yet been builded that could express my joy.

The chancel is sweet with bride roses—I have seen it this afternoon—and vines are swinging everywhere. There will be lights and the Lohengrin music, but I shall see nothing but your face, hear nothing but your soft, dreamy voice, saying over after that blessed Bishop the things he will ask you to say, and when he bids me seal the compact, I know but too well that the lights will go out for me and that I shall have only your lips in the dark.

Sweet, brave little soul, can you trust yourself to me for all the years to come ? It is not a promise, but a consecration, when I say that you have placed your faith aright.

Since I began to talk to you, another hour has flown by, and I must bring this letter to a close. It is the last I can ever write you, for I am never going to leave your side again.

Because I love you, better than all the world beside, I shall hold your hand in mine till one of us is summoned, and if that one be you, I shall follow, through whatever countries you may go, and at the end of your journey hold you fast, for forever and a day.

THE END

www.ingramcontent.com/pod-product-compliance
Lightning Source LLC
Chambersburg PA
CBHW020228030726
47497CB00009B/2999